Kenneth Grahame

The Wind in the Willows

楊柳風

U0108769

商務印書館

This Chinese edition of *The Wind in the Willows* has been published with the written permission of Black Cat Publishing.

The copyright of this Chinese edition is owned by The Commercial Press (H.K.) Ltd.

Name of Book: The Wind in the Willows
Author: Kenneth Grahame
Editors: Rober Hill
Design and art direction: Nadia Maestri
Computer graphics: Sara Blasigh
Illustrations: Giovanni Manna
Picture research: Laura Lagomarsino
Edition: ©2006 Black Cat Publishing,
　　　　an imprint of Cideb Editrice, Genoa, Canterbury

系 列 名：Black Cat 優質英語階梯閱讀 · Level 1
書　　名：楊柳風
責任編輯：畢　琦
封面設計：張　毅
出　　版：商務印書館（香港）有限公司
　　　　　香港筲箕灣耀興道 3 號東滙廣場 8 樓
　　　　　http://www.commercialpress.com.hk
發　　行：香港聯合書刊物流有限公司
　　　　　香港新界大埔汀麗路 36 號中華商務印刷大廈 3 字樓
印　　刷：中華商務彩色印刷有限公司
　　　　　香港新界大埔汀麗路36號中華商務印刷大廈
版　　次：2006年 11月第 1版第 1次印刷
　　　　　© 2006 商務印書館（香港）有限公司
　　　　　ISBN 13 - 978 962 07 1776 5
　　　　　ISBN 10 - 962 07 1776 7
　　　　　Printed in Hong Kong

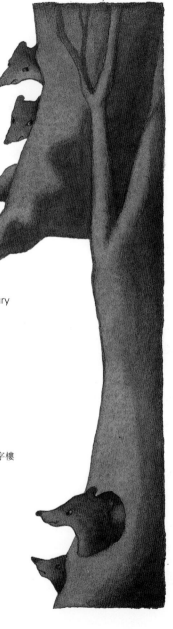

出版説明

　　本館一向倡導優質閱讀，近年來連續推出了以 "Q" 為標識的 "Quality English Learning 優質英語學習" 系列，其中《讀名著學英語》叢書，更是香港書展入選好書，讀者反響令人鼓舞。推動社會閱讀風氣，推動英語經典閱讀，藉閱讀拓廣世界視野，提高英語水平，已經成為一種潮流。

　　然良好閱讀習慣的養成非一日之功，大多數初中級程度的讀者，常視直接閱讀厚重的原著為畏途。如何給年輕的讀者提供切實的指引和幫助，如何既提供優質的學習素材，又提供名師的教學方法，是當下社會關注的重要問題。　針對這種情況，本館特別延請香港名校名師，根據多年豐富的教學經驗，精選海外適合初中級英語程度讀者的優質經典讀物，有系統地出版了這套叢書，名為《Black Cat 優質英語階梯閱讀》。

　　《Black Cat 優質英語階梯閱讀》體現了香港名校名師堅持經典學習的教學理念，以及多年行之有效的學習方法。既有經過改寫和縮寫的經典名著，又有富創意的現代作品；既有精心設計的聽、説、讀、寫綜合練習，又有豐富的歷史文化知識；既有彩色插圖、繪圖和照片，又有英美專業演員朗讀作品的 CD。適合口味不同的讀者享受閱讀之樂，欣賞經典之美。

　　《Black Cat 優質英語階梯閱讀》由淺入深，逐階提升，好像參與一個尋寶遊戲，入門並不難，但要真正尋得寶藏，需要投入，更需要堅持。只有置身其中的人，才能體味純正英語的魅力，領略得到真寶的快樂。當英語閱讀成為自己生活的一部分，英語水平的提高自然水到渠成。

商務印書館 (香港) 有限公司
編輯部

使用說明

① 應該怎樣選書？

按閱讀興趣選書

《Black Cat 優質英語階梯閱讀》精選世界經典作品，也包括富於創意的現代作品；既有膾炙人口的小說、戲劇，又有非小說類的文化知識讀物，品種豐富，內容多樣，適合口味不同的讀者挑選自己感興趣的書，享受閱讀的樂趣。

按英語程度選書

《Black Cat 優質英語階梯閱讀》現設 Level 1 至 Level 6，由淺入深，涵蓋初、中級英語程度。讀物分級採用了國際上通用的劃分標準，主要以詞彙（vocabulary）和結構（structures）劃分。

Level 1 至 Level 3 出現的詞彙較淺顯，相對深的核心詞彙均配上中文解釋，節省讀者查找詞典的時間，以專心理解正文內容。在註釋的幫助下，讀者若能流暢地閱讀正文內容，就不用擔心這一本書程度過深。

Level 1 至 Level 3 出現的動詞時態形式和句子結構比較簡單。動詞時態形式以現在時（present simple）、現在時進行式（present continuous）、過去時（past simple）為主，句子結構大部分是簡單句（simple sentences）。此外，還包括比較級和最高級（comparative and superlative forms）、可數和不可數名詞（countable and uncountable nouns）以及冠詞（articles）等語法知識點。

Level 4 至 Level 6 出現的的動詞時態形式，以現在完成時（present perfect）、現在完成時進行式（present perfect continuous）、過去完成時（past perfect continuous）為主，句子結構大部分是複合句（compound sentences）、條件從句（1st and 2nd conditional sentences）等。此外，還包括情態動詞（modal verbs）、被動形式（passive forms）、動名詞

(gerunds)、短語動詞（phrasal verbs）等語法知識點。

　　根據上述的語法範圍，讀者可按自己實際的英語水平，如詞彙量、語法知識、理解能力、閱讀能力等自主選擇，不再受制於學校年級劃分或學歷高低的約束，完全根據個人需要選擇合適的讀物。

② 怎樣提高閱讀效果？

　　閱讀的方法主要有兩種：一是泛讀，二是精讀。兩者各有功能，適當地結合使用，相輔相成，有事半功倍之效。

　　泛讀，指閱讀大量適合自己程度（可稍淺，但不能過深）、不同內容、風格、體裁的讀物，但求明白內容大意，不用花費太多時間鑽研細節，主要作用是多接觸英語，減輕對它的生疏感，鞏固以前所學過的英語，讓腦子在潛意識中吸收詞彙用法、語法結構等。

　　精讀，指小心認真地閱讀內容精彩、組織有條理、遣詞造句又正確的作品，着重點在於理解"準確"及"深入"，欣賞其精彩獨到之處。精讀時，可充分利用書中精心設計的練習，學習掌握有用的英語詞彙和語法知識。精讀後，可再花十分鐘朗讀其中一小段有趣的文字，邊唸邊細心領會文字的結構和意思。

　　《Black Cat 優質英語階梯閱讀》中的作品均值得精讀，如時間有限，不妨嘗試每兩個星期泛讀一本，輔以每星期挑選書中一章精彩的文字精讀。要學好英語，持之以恆地泛讀和精讀英文是最有效的方法。

③ 本系列的練習與測試有何功能？

　　《Black Cat 優質英語階梯閱讀》特別注重練習的設計，為讀者考慮周到，切合實用需求，學習功能強。每章後均配有訓練聽、說、讀、寫四項技能的練習，分量、難度恰到好處。

聽力練習分兩類，一是重聽故事回答問題，二是聆聽主角對話、書信朗讀、或模擬記者訪問後寫出答案，旨在以生活化的練習形式逐步提高聽力。每本書均配有 CD 提供作品朗讀，朗讀者都是專業演員，英國作品由英國演員錄音，美國作品由美國演員錄音，務求增加聆聽的真實感和感染力。多聆聽英式和美式英語兩種發音，可讓讀者熟悉二者的差異，逐漸培養分辨英美發音的能力，提高聆聽理解的準確度。此外，模仿錄音朗讀故事或模仿主人翁在戲劇中的對白，都是訓練口語能力的好方法。

閱讀理解練習形式多樣化，有縱橫字謎、配對、填空、字句重組等等，注重訓練讀者的理解、推敲和聯想等多種閱讀技能。

寫作練習尤具新意，教讀者使用網式圖示（spidergrams）記錄重點，採用問答、書信、電報、記者採訪等多樣化形式，鼓勵讀者動手寫作。

書後更設有升級測試（Exit Test）及答案，供讀者檢查學習效果。充分利用書中的練習和測試，可全面提升聽、說、讀、寫四項技能。

④ 本系列還能提供甚麼幫助？

《Black Cat 優質英語階梯閱讀》提倡豐富多元的現代閱讀，巧用書中提供的資訊，有助於提升英語理解力，擴闊視野。

每本書都設有專章介紹相關的歷史文化知識，經典名著更有作者生平、社會背景等資訊。書內富有表現力的彩色插圖、繪圖和照片，使閱讀充滿趣味，部分加上如何解讀古典名畫的指導，增長見識。有的書還提供一些與主題相關的網址，比如關於不同國家的節慶源流的網址，讓讀者多利用網上資源增進知識。

CONTENTS

The text is recorded in full.　故事錄音

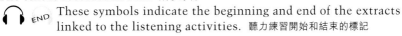 END　These symbols indicate the beginning and end of the extracts
linked to the listening activities.　聽力練習開始和結束的標記

About the Author

Name: Kenneth Grahame

Born: Edinburgh, Scotland

Date: 8 March 1859

Job: banker

Most famous book: *The Wind in the Willows* (1908)

Reason for writing *The Wind in the Willows*: for his son Alistair

Other books: *Pagan Papers* (1893), *The Golden Age* (1895), *Dream Days* (1898)

Died: 6 July 1932

Meet the Characters

Mole

Rat

Badger

Toad

GLOSSARY

1 **Here are the names of all the animals in the story. Do you know them?**

mole

rabbit

horse

otter

badger

toad

squirrel

weasel

fox

bird

water rat

kingfisher

moorhen

stoat

ferret

2 Do you know these words? Write the words from the box next to the correct picture. Use your dictionary to help you.

meadow
wood
sunlight
grass
river
river bank
willow

3 Now find the words in the word square.

M	E	A	D	O	W	A	I
S	A	T	E	W	O	I	D
R	U	O	S	O	O	D	N
I	R	N	C	L	D	C	K
V	I	A	L	L	R	Y	A
E	V	T	P	I	O	F	F
R	E	O	U	W	G	T	X
H	R	E	U	O	R	H	M
E	B	S	P	I	A	C	T
R	A	V	M	A	S	R	C
W	N	P	U	N	S	V	A
R	K	I	F	D	A	P	N

CHAPTER 1

THE RIVER BANK

t is spring and the Mole is cleaning his little home. He is working very hard and he is very tired. Suddenly he decides to stop. He wants to go outside. He goes up a small tunnel and arrives outside in a meadow.

"This is nice!" he thinks when he arrives in the sunlight, "This is better than cleaning!" He is very happy.

He crosses meadows and woods. He sees rabbits, birds and a lot of other animals. They are all working hard. Finally he arrives at the river. He sits down on the grass.

The Water Rat comes out of his hole in the river bank. He sees Mole.

"Hello, Mole," he says, "Would you like to come over?"

"Hello, Rat. Yes, I would. But how?" replies Mole.

"I can come and get you in my boat." Rat gets into a little

boat and crosses the river. Mole gets into the boat.

"This is wonderful!" says Mole, "This is my first time in a boat."

"Your first time!" says Rat, "There's nothing better than boats! Let's go for a picnic."

"Oh, yes please!" says Mole.

THE WIND IN THE WILLOWS

Rat goes into his house and returns with a big basket full of food. They go down the river in the boat. Rat tells Mole about life on the river and about his neighbours [1] – the otters, [2] kingfishers [3] and moorhens. [4]

Mole sees a wood in the distance.

"What's over there?" he asks.

"That's the Wild Wood," says Rat, "We don't go there often."

"Are they nice people there?" asks Mole.

"Well," replies Rat, "the squirrels and rabbits are alright. And there's Badger. He's nice. But the weasels, stoats and foxes... you must be careful with them."

They stop for their picnic and Mole unpacks the basket. Soon the Otter arrives.

"Hello, Otter," says Rat, "This is my friend Mr Mole."

"Pleased to meet you," says Otter to Mole.

Suddenly the Badger appears and Rat invites him to the picnic. But Badger turns around and goes away.

"Badger hates company!" says Rat, "We don't see him often. But look! There's Toad on the river in his new boat."

"It's Toad's new hobby," says Otter.

"Yes," says Rat, "First it was sailing. Then it was houseboating. [5] He changes hobby all the time."

Rat waves to Toad but Toad doesn't stop.

Rat and Mole return to Rat's house in the boat. Rat invites Mole to stay with him and Mole is very happy.

---

1. **neighbours**：鄰居。
2. **otters**：水獺。
3. **kingfishers**：翠鳥。

4. **moorhens**：水雞。

5. **houseboating**：

UNDERSTANDING THE TEXT

1 **Are these sentences "Right" (A) or "Wrong" (B)? If there is not enough information to answer "Right" or "Wrong", choose "Doesn't say" (C).**

0   Mole is cleaning his house.
    ⒶRight   **B** Wrong   **C** Doesn't say

1   He leaves his house and walks to the river.
    A Right   **B** Wrong   **C** Doesn't say

2   Water Rat invites Mole into his house.
    A Right   **B** Wrong   **C** Doesn't say

3   Mole is very happy to go on the boat.
    A Right   **B** Wrong   **C** Doesn't say

4   Rat tells Mole about the Wild Wood.
    A Right   **B** Wrong   **C** Doesn't say

5   They eat a lot at the picnic.
    A Right   **B** Wrong   **C** Doesn't say

6   Badger doesn't like to be with other people.
    A Right   **B** Wrong   **C** Doesn't say

7   Toad comes to the picnic.
    A Right   **B** Wrong   **C** Doesn't say

8   Mole is sad to stay with Rat.
    A Right   **B** Wrong   **C** Doesn't say

2 **Complete the conversations. Choose A, B or C.**

1   Would you like to come to my house? **A** ☐ Yes, thank you.
                                              B ☐ No, I don't.
                                              C ☐ No, thank you.

2   Pleased to meet you.   **A** ☐ Hello.
                               B ☐ Pleased to meet you.
                               C ☐ Yes, me too.

3   Let's go swimming.   **A** ☐ Good idea!
                              B ☐ No, let's don't.
                              C ☐ Yes, let's.

SCRAMBLED WORDS

A   Unscramble the words in the box and write them in the centre of the spidergrams.

1 psrign   2 neitwr   3 mutuna   4 mursem

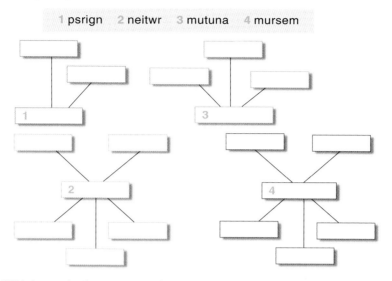

B   Which words do you associate with the seasons? Use the words in the box to complete the spidergrams.

cold   hot   flowers   rain   beach   swimming   ice cream
holidays   ice skating   skiing   coats   snow   leaves   gold   yellow

C   Now match the season to the correct part of the picture.

CHAPTER 2

THE OPEN ROAD

ne summer morning Mole and Rat decide to
visit Mr Toad, They get in the boat and go up
the river.

"Toad's rich, you know," says Rat.

"Is Toad very nice?" asks Mole.

"Oh yes!" replies Rat, "He's very nice. He isn't very intelligent – but
we can't all be clever. And sometimes he's boastful [1] and arrogant. [2]
But he's got some good qualities."

Soon they arrive at Toad Hall. They pass by a boating house. It is
full of boats. They are all out of the water.

"It seems that Toad isn't interested in boating anymore. I wonder [3]
what his new hobby is," says Rat.

Rat and Mole get out of the boat and walk across the gardens of

---

1. **boastful** : 自誇的。
2. **arrogant** : 自大的。
3. **wonder** : 想知道。

THE OPEN ROAD

Toad Hall. They see Toad in the garden. He is looking at a big map. He is very pleased to see Rat and Mole.

"Hello, Toad," says Rat, "This is my friend Mole."

"Oh, splendid!" cries Toad, "Pleased to meet you. Come and see my new hobby."

He shows them a gypsy caravan. [1] It is yellow and green with red wheels.

"There's real life!" cries Toad, "The open road: travel, change, interest, excitement! Look inside – everything's there. We've got

1. **gypsy caravan**：吉卜賽篷車。

everything for our journey this afternoon."

"Excuse me – you say 'we', 'our', 'this afternoon'?" asks Rat.

"Yes, Ratty. I can't go without you," says Toad.

"Oh, Rat – it's so exciting!" says Mole.

"Very well," says Rat, "Let's go!"

After lunch, they go to the paddock [1] and catch the old grey horse. Then they set off on the road. It is a lovely afternoon and the birds whistle at them and passers-by say, "good afternoon". In the evening they stop and eat a simple meal. Then they go to bed. The next morning Toad sleeps until very late so Mole walks to the nearest village. He buys milk and eggs for breakfast, and Rat lights a fire and washes the dinner plates from the night before. They are very tired after this hard work. Finally Toad gets up.

"Life on the road is very easy," he says.

After breakfast they set off. They are walking along the road when suddenly a magnificent motorcar drives past. The horse is frightened and pulls the caravan off the road into a ditch. [2] The caravan is ruined!

Rat is furious. "You villains! [3] Police! Help!" he shouts.

But Toad is sitting in the middle of the road. He is staring in the direction of the motorcar. "Poop poop!" he says, "Poop poop!"

Rat and Mole try to pull the caravan out of the ditch but they can"t.

Rat asks, "Can you help us, Toad?"

"Poop poop!" replies Toad, "Now that's the real way to travel – the only way."

The caravan is ruined and they must return home by train. The next day Toad buys a big and very expensive motorcar.

1. **paddock** : 圍場。

2. **ditch** : 溝渠。

3. **villains** : 壞人。

UNDERSTANDING THE TEXT

KET

1 Choose A, B, or C.

0 Mole and Rat decide to visit
  A ✔ Toad.
  B ☐ Badger.
  C ☐ Otter.

1 Toad is
  A ☐ intelligent and arrogant.
  B ☐ rich and boastful.
  C ☐ clever and nice.

2 The boating house is
  A ☐ empty.
  B ☐ full of boats.
  C ☐ full of water.

3 What is Toad looking at?
  A ☐ a caravan
  B ☐ a map
  C ☐ a garden

4 Toad's new hobby is
  A ☐ travelling by caravan.
  B ☐ gypsies.
  C ☐ horses.

5 Who sleeps until very late?
  A ☐ Mole
  B ☐ Rat
  C ☐ Toad

6 The horse is frightened by
  A ☐ the motorcar.
  B ☐ the ditch.
  C ☐ the caravan.

7 The caravan
  A ☐ falls into the ditch.
  B ☐ crashes into the motorcar.
  C ☐ pulls the horse into the ditch.

8 Mole, Rat and Toad return home by
  A ☐ motorcar.
  B ☐ train.
  C ☐ caravan.

T: GRADE 2

2 SPEAKING
Topic – Home
Toad lives in a very big house. Describe your home. Use these questions to help you.

1 Do you live in a house or a flat?
2 Is it old or modern?
3 How many rooms are there?
4 How many bedrooms has it got?
5 Which is your favourite room?
6 Who lives in your home with you?

CHAPTER 3

THE WILD WOOD

ole wants to meet Badger.

"Could you ask him here for dinner?" he asks Rat.

"He wouldn't come," replies Rat, "He hates company."

"Well, can we go and call on him?" suggests Mole.

"Oh no," says Rat, "He's very shy. And also he lives in the middle of the Wild Wood."

It is clear that Rat doesn't want to visit Badger.

It is winter time and Rat sleeps a lot. One afternoon he is sleeping in his armchair in front of the fire, so Mole decides to go and explore the Wild Wood and meet Badger. He goes outside. It is very cold and the sky is grey. He is happy, and when he arrives at the Wild Wood he is not frightened.

THE WIND IN THE WILLOWS

Then he starts to see faces — hundreds of faces; little faces with hard eyes. Mole is frightened and leaves the path. [1] In a panic [2] Mole starts to run — he doesn't know where. Finally he hides inside the hollow of an old tree.

Rat wakes up and looks for Mole. But Mole is not there. Mole's hat and boots are gone. Rat goes outside and sees footprints. [3] They are going in the direction of the Wild Wood. Rat is worried. He goes back into the house, takes two pistols [4] and a big stick [5] and sets off for the Wild Wood.

He also sees little faces with hard eyes, but they disappear

1. **path** : 小徑。
2. **panic** : 恐慌。
3. **footprints** :
4. **pistols** : 手槍。
5. **stick** :

immediately when they see his pistols and stick. Rat hunts for an hour, "Moly, Moly! Where are you? It's me – Rat!"

Finally he hears a cry, "Ratty! Is that really you? I'm so frightened!"

Rat sees Mole under the tree. "Mole, you mustn't come into the Wild Wood alone. We animals from the river bank always come in couples."

"But brave Mr Toad isn't frightened of the wood," says Mole.

Rat laughs, "Toad!? He wouldn't come here for a hat full of gold. But now we must leave for home before night comes."

Rat looks around. "It's snowing! And everything looks so different in the snow."

They set off bravely but after two hours they stop for a rest. The snow is very deep and they are very tired and wet.

"We're very tired," says Rat, "Let's find a dry cave [1] or hole. Then we can rest before trying again."

They look for shelter. [2] Suddenly Mole falls down. "Oh, my leg!" he cries.

"Poor Mole!" says Rat. He looks at the cut on Mole's leg. "This is a cut from metal not a branch," [3] he says. He starts to dig in the snow.

"Hooray! Hooray!" he shouts.

"What is it?!" asks Mole.

They see a little green door. A bell [4] is hanging next to it. Under the bell is written "Mr Badger". Rat hits the door with his stick and Mole rings the bell.

1. **cave** :
2. **shelter** : 藏身處。

3. **branch** : 樹枝。
4. **bell** :

UNDERSTANDING THE TEXT

 Answer the following questions.

1 Who does Mole want to meet?
2 Why does Rat sleep a lot?
3 Why is Mole frightened in the wood?
4 What does Rat take with him to the wood?
5 What is the weather like?
6 What do Mole and Rat find?

 Read the descriptions of some weather words. What is the correct word (A-H) for each description?

		ANSWER
0	You need this for skiing.	A
1	You can't see very well in this.	......
2	This is frozen rain.	......
3	You carry an umbrella for this.	......
4	If you go sailing, you need this.	......
5	You want this if you go to the beach.	......

A snow	**C** rain	**E** cloud	**G** wind
B fog	**D** hail	**F** sunshine	**H** storm

T: GRADE 2

 SPEAKING
Topic – Friends
Mole and Rat are now good friends. Describe your best friend. Use the following questions to help you.

1 Is your friend a boy or a girl?
2 What is your friend called?
3 How old is your friend?
4 What does he/she look like?
5 What do like about your friend?

28

Animals in Winter

🎧 In winter time it gets cold, snow covers the ground and there is no food. So how do animals survive?

Migration

Many birds, fish and other animals migrate in the autumn. They travel south to warmer places and then return in the spring.

Adaptation

Some animals like the mole stay and remain active in the winter months. To keep warm they may grow new, thicker fur in autumn. Because food is difficult to find, some animals like mice and squirrels collect extra food and store it to eat later.

Hibernation

Some animals such as the rat hibernate during the winter. This is a special, very deep sleep. The animal's body temperature goes down and its heartbeat and breathing slow down. In the autumn these animals prepare by eating extra food, which is stored as body fat and can be used as energy during the winter.

 Read the descriptions of some words from the text. What is the correct word for each description?

1   hair that grows on the body of animals

   ....

2   move at a particular time or season from one part of the world to another

   ....

3   ability and strength to do active physical things

   ....

4   put away and keep until needed

   ....

5   deep sleep during the winter

   ....

6   regular movement of your heart

   ....

BEFORE YOU READ

1 **Listen to the first part of Chapter 4 and choose the correct answer A, B or C.**

1 Badger opens the door
   A ☐ immediately.
   B ☐ after a long time.
   C ☐ after a short time.

2 Badger takes them to the
   A ☐ kitchen.
   B ☐ living room.
   C ☐ bathroom.

3 Mole and Rat are
   A ☐ very angry.
   B ☐ very hungry.
   C ☐ very tired.

4 Toad
   A ☐ is a good driver.
   B ☐ has a lot of accidents.
   C ☐ is sensible.

5 Rat and Mole's bedroom is full of
   A ☐ furniture.
   B ☐ food.
   C ☐ drink.

2 **SCRAMBLED ADJECTIVES**
Unscramble the adjectives and then use the words to fill the gaps in the sentences.

A grayn
B bessnile
C elpyse
D ypaph
E ogdo

1 Badger is .... when he opens the door.
2 Toad thinks that he is a .... driver.
3 Toad isn't very ....
4 Rat and Mole are .... so they go to bed.
5 Mole is .... to return home.

CHAPTER 4

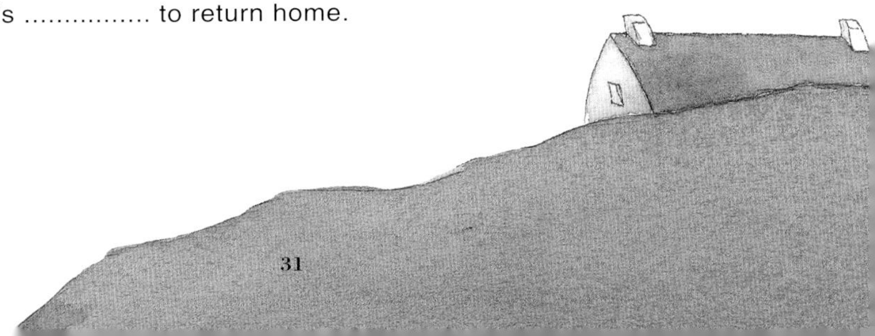

MR BADGER

ole and Rat wait for a long time and finally 🎧 they hear footsteps. The door opens a little and they see a nose and two sleepy eyes.

"Who is it?" asks Badger. He is angry.

"Oh, Badger!" cries Rat, "It's me, Rat and my friend Mole. We're lost in the snow."

"My dear Ratty!" says Badger, "Come in. Lost in the snow! In the Wild Wood! This isn't the kind of night for small animals to be out."

He takes them to the kitchen. There is a fire burning in the fireplace. Badger gives them dressing gowns and slippers. They sit in front of the fire while Badger prepares dinner for them. They are very hungry and they eat and eat.

"How's old Toad?" asks Badger.

"From bad to worse," says Rat, " – another accident in his car. This

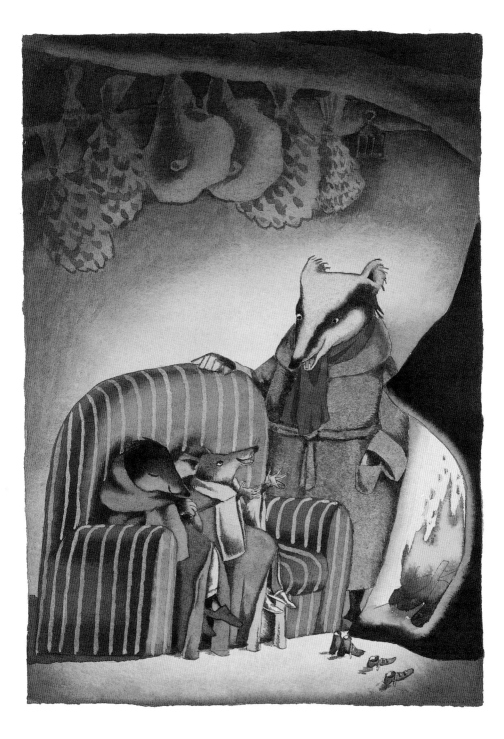

THE WIND IN THE WILLOWS

is the seventh. He's always in hospital or paying fines. [1] He needs to pay for a driver but he's convinced that he's a good driver!"

Badger thinks. "I can't do anything now. But when the nights are short we must talk to Toad. He must become sensible! Now it's time for bed."

He takes them to a room. It is full of food for the winter – apples, turnips, potatoes, nuts and honey. But there are also two little beds. Mole and Rat get undressed and go to sleep.

END

The next morning they get up very late. They are eating breakfast in the kitchen when the front door bell rings. It's Otter. He is very happy to see Rat and Mole.

"Everybody on the river is very worried about you," he says.

At that moment Badger arrives. "I think it's time for lunch," he says.

During lunch Otter and Rat talk about the river. Mole tells Badger, "I like your house. It's good to live underground."

Badger is pleased that Mole likes his house. "Yes, here it's safe, peaceful and quiet."

After lunch Badger shows Mole his home. There are a lot of rooms and tunnels. [2] They return to the kitchen. Ratty is wearing his coat. "Come on, Mole. It's time to go," he says, "We must go before night." He is worried.

"It's alright," says Otter, "I'm coming with you."

"Don't worry, Ratty," says Badger, "My tunnels go to the edge [3] of the wood." He picks up a lantern [4] and takes them down a long tunnel. After a long time they see daylight. They are on the edge of the Wild Wood. Badger says goodbye and goes away quickly. Otter takes them to the river. Mole is very happy to be home.

---

1. **fines**：罰款。
2. **tunnels**：隧道。
3. **edge**：邊緣。
4. **lantern**：燈籠。

UNDERSTANDING THE TEXT

1 Are these sentences "Right" (A) or "Wrong" (B)? If there is not enough information to answer "Right" or "Wrong", choose "Doesn't say" (C).

0 Badger is sleeping when Rat and Mole knock on the door.
  (A) Right   **B** Wrong   **C** Doesn't say

1 Rat and Mole are lost.
  A Right   **B** Wrong   **C** Doesn't say

2 Badger invites Rat and Mole into his house.
  A Right   **B** Wrong   **C** Doesn't say

3 Badger eats dinner with Rat and Mole.
  A Right   **B** Wrong   **C** Doesn't say

4 Badger wants to help Toad immediately.
  A Right   **B** Wrong   **C** Doesn't say

5 The next morning they get up early.
  A Right   **B** Wrong   **C** Doesn't say

6 Rat and Mole leave after breakfast.
  A Right   **B** Wrong   **C** Doesn't say

2 **QUESTION WORDS**
Use the question words in the box to fill the gaps in the sentences.

> who   when   where   why   how

1 "............. is it?" "It's me."

2 "............. are you?" "I'm fine, thanks."

3 "............. are Mole and Rat?" "They're in the Wild Wood."

4 "............. does Badger want to talk to Toad?" "In the summer."

5 "............. must they talk to Toad?" "Because he must become sensible."

CHAPTER **5**

MR TOAD

 t is a sunny morning in summer. Mole and Rat are having breakfast. Suddenly there is a knock at the door.

Mole goes to the door and comes back with Badger. Badger looks very serious.

"It's time!" he says.

"Time for what?" asks Rat. He looks at the clock.

"Time for *who*!" says Badger, "Time for Toad. We must talk to him. I know that another big new motorcar is arriving at Toad Hall today. We must go and talk to Toad before it's too late!"

"Good!" says Rat, "We must save poor Toad!"

When they arrive at Toad Hall a big red car is in front of the house. Toad is coming out of the house. He is wearing goggles, [1] a cap, an enormous coat and gloves. [2]

"Hello!" he says when he sees them.

"Take him inside," says Badger to Rat and Mole. They take him inside.

1. **goggles**：護目鏡。　　　2. **gloves**：手套。

"Now, Toad," says Badger, "take these stupid clothes off."

"No!" says Toad, "Why are you doing this?"

"Take his clothes off," Badger orders. Rat sits on Toad, and Mole takes off Toad's motor clothes.

"Now, Toad," says Badger, "you don't listen to our advice. [1] You are spending all your money. And people are talking about the animals because of your fast driving and problems with the police."

But Toad is not sorry. So they lock him in a bedroom.

"You can come out when you're sorry," says Rat. They go downstairs. Toad shouts at them through the keyhole.

"Toad's very determined," says Badger, "It's a difficult situation. We must never leave Toad alone."

The days pass but Toad is still interested in cars. He becomes depressed. [2]

One morning Rat is with Toad. "How are you today, Toad?" he asks.

"Not very well," replies Toad, "Could you go to the village and call the doctor?"

Rat is worried. "A doctor! He must be very ill." He goes out of the room and locks the door. Then he runs to the village.

Toad jumps out of bed and laughs. He gets dressed quickly. He puts some money in his pockets. He climbs out of the window and jumps to the ground. He then walks away in the opposite direction [3] to Rat. The sun is shining and he is very happy with himself. "Poor Ratty," he thinks, "he's a very good animal but not very intelligent. I must educate him one day."

He arrives in a small town and sees a sign: "The Red Lion". Toad is very hungry. He goes into the inn [4] and orders a big lunch. Suddenly

1. **advice** : 忠告。
2. **depressed** : 沮丧。
3. **opposite direction** : 相反的方向。
4. **inn** : 小酒店。

he hears "poop poop" and sees a car outside the inn. The people get out and go into the inn. Toad walks outside. He looks at the car.

"I wonder," he thinks, "if this type of car starts easily."

In a dream, he starts the car, then sits in the driver's seat and drives away. He doesn't think about right or wrong. He drives faster and faster.

"We must punish this villain severely," says the magistrate. "He's guilty, [1] first of all, of stealing [2] a motorcar, secondly of driving dangerously, and thirdly of being rude [3] to the police. I give you twenty years in prison!"

Poor Toad is locked up in prison!

1. **guilty** : 有罪的。
2. **stealing** : 偷。
3. **being rude** : 粗鲁。

UNDERSTANDING THE TEXT

1 **Choose A, B, or C.**

1 Badger wants to talk to Toad before
 A ☐ it is too early.
 B ☐ it is too late.
 C ☐ it is time.

2 When they arrive at Toad Hall, Toad is
 A ☐ leaving.
 B ☐ arriving.
 C ☐ waiting for them.

3 Why do they lock Toad in his bedroom?
 A ☐ Because he is angry.
 B ☐ Because he isn't sorry.
 C ☐ Because he shouts at them.

4 Toad tells Rat that
 A ☐ he is ill.
 B ☐ he is interested in cars.
 C ☐ he wants to go to the village.

5 Toad thinks that he is very
 A ☐ intelligent.
 B ☐ ill.
 C ☐ worried.

6 Why does Toad take the car?
 A ☐ Because he wants to drive it.
 B ☐ Because he thinks about right or wrong.
 C ☐ Because he wants to return home.

7 Toad is found guilty of
 A ☐ one crime.
 B ☐ two crimes.
 C ☐ three crimes.

2 **WRITING**
Complete Toad's letter to Badger, Rat and Mole. Write one word for each space.

Dear Badger, Rat and Mole,

I (1)............ in trouble! I am now (2)............ prison for stealing (3)............ car. The prison is very cold (4)............ damp and I am alone in my cell. I am (5)............ unhappy. (6)............ am very sorry for escaping. You (7)............ all very intelligent and sensible. Please help (8)............ .
I hope you can (9)............ something.

Love
Toad

40

3 THE TIME

Look at the clocks and write down the time. When possible write each time in two ways.

1 ....
....

2 ....
....

3 ....
....

4 ....
....

5 ....
....

6 ....
....

TOAD'S ADVENTURES

oad is very unhappy. "This is the end of everything," he thinks, "the end of the career of Toad, the popular and handsome Toad, the rich and kind Toad."

He starts crying. "Now I must stay in this dark prison. Oh clever Rat and sensible Mole. Oh intelligent Badger!"

Poor Toad! The days and weeks pass and he refuses [1] to eat.

The gaoler [2] has got a daughter and she helps her father in the prison. She is very fond of [3] animals and is sorry for Toad. One day she asks, "Father, please let me look after Toad. He's so unhappy and so thin."

She knocks on the door of Toad's cell.

1. **refuses**：拒絕。
2. **gaoler**：典獄長。
3. **is very fond of**：非常喜歡。

"Now, Toad," she says, "sit up and stop crying. Be sensible and eat some dinner."

The dinner smells very good and Toad starts to think that life is not so bad. He sits up and starts to eat. The gaoler's daughter asks him about Toad Hall. He talks about his home. Then she asks him about his animal friends. When the girl leaves Toad is himself again – the same arrogant animal.

The days pass and they have a lot of interesting talks together. The gaoler's daughter is very sorry for Toad and thinks it is wrong that Toad is in prison. Vain [1] Toad believes that she is in love with him and is a little sorry that the social gap [2] between them is so big.

One morning she says, "Listen Toad, I've got an aunt. She's a washerwoman [3] and does the washing for all the prisoners here. Now, you're very rich and she's very poor. I think that if you pay her she can give you her dress and bonnet [4] and you can escape. You are very similar."

"We are not!" says Toad, "I'm very elegant, considering I'm a toad."

"My aunt's also elegant, considering she's a washerwoman," says the girl, "I'm trying to help you and you are proud [5] and ungrateful!" [6]

"Please introduce me to your aunt," says Toad.

The next evening the girl's aunt comes into the cell. She is carrying Toad's washing. On the table is a pile of gold coins. [7] The washerwoman gives Toad a cotton dress, an apron and a bonnet. Then Toad takes off his coat and waistcoat and puts on the dress, apron and bonnet.

"Goodbye, Toad," says the girl.

1. **vain** : 自負的。
2. **social gap** : 社會差距。
3. **washerwoman** : 洗衣婦。
4. **bonnet** : 女帽。
5. **proud** : 驕傲的。
6. **ungrateful** : 不領情的。
7. **coins** :

TOAD'S ADVENTURES

Toad is nervous, but he goes out. No one stops him. When he is outside he walks towards the town. Soon he sees some red and green lights and the noise of a train. "Aha!" he thinks, "A railway station. I can catch a train home!"

He goes to the ticket office and asks for a ticket to the village near Toad Hall. But he has no money! It is all in his waistcoat pocket in the prison. He cannot get home!

Toad is very sad. He walks down the platform. He starts to cry.

"Hello, what's the matter?" asks the train driver.

"Oh, sir!" cries Toad, "I'm a poor washerwoman. I have no money. I can't pay for a ticket and I must get home tonight."

"Very well," says the kind train driver, "You're a washerwoman. I can give you a ride if you wash some shirts for me."

Toad climbs up. The guard waves his flag [1] and the train moves out of the station. Now Toad is very happy. He thinks about Toad Hall, his friends and good things to eat.

After some time the train driver says, "It's very strange. We're the last train tonight but I'm sure there's another train behind us."

Toad immediately becomes serious and depressed.

"And the train is full of policemen with truncheons. [2] They're shouting 'Stop! Stop! Stop!'" continues the train driver.

Toad falls to his knees. "Save me, Mr train driver. I'm not a washerwoman. I'm Toad – the well-known and popular Mr Toad. They want me. I'm a car thief and I'm running away from prison."

The train driver looks very serious. "I must stop and give you to the police. But you're obviously very sorry. Soon there's a tunnel. At the other end there's a wood. You must jump out and hide in the wood."

After the tunnel Toad jumps. He runs into the wood and hides.

1. **flag** :   2. **truncheons** : 警棍。

45

The Wind in the Willows

The police train comes out of the tunnel and continues following the other train.

Toad laughs. But soon he stops laughing. It is very late and dark and cold. He is in a strange wood with no money and far away from

friends and home. Cold, hungry and tired he makes a bed with dead
leaves [1] and branches under a tree and goes to sleep.

1. **leaves** :

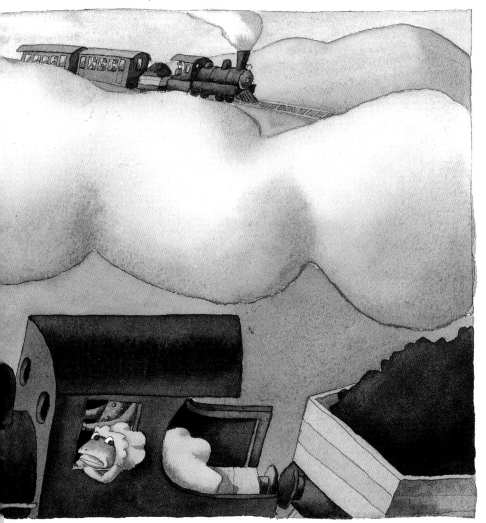

UNDERSTANDING THE TEXT

 Answer the following questions.

1 Why does the gaoler's daughter want to look after Toad?
2 What does Toad talk about with the girl?
3 What does Toad think about the girl?
4 What does the washerwoman give to Toad?
5 What does Toad give to the washerwoman?
6 Why does Toad start crying?
7 Why does the train driver help Toad?
8 Where does Toad jump off the train?

 VOCABULARY
Label the clothes with words from the box.

> dress jacket waistcoat apron goggles bonnet
> coat trousers shirt gloves shoes

1 ....
2 ....
3 ....
4 ....
5 ....
6 ....
7 ....
8 ....
9 ....
10 ....
11 ....

CHAPTER 7

THE FURTHER ADVENTURES OF TOAD

oad wakes up early. The sun is shining. He stands up and starts walking. Soon he sees a canal. On it there is a barge [1] pulled by a horse. There is a woman on the barge.

"Good morning," she says to Toad.

"Maybe it's good for you," says Toad, "but I'm a poor washerwoman and I am going to see my married daughter. She's in trouble. [2] All my other children are alone. I'm lost with no money."

"Where does your daughter live?" asks the barge woman.

"Near the river," replies Toad, "near a fine house called Toad Hall."

---

1. **barge** : 駁船。   2. **in trouble** : 有麻煩。

"Toad Hall? I'm going in that direction," says the woman, "Come with me in the barge. I can take you near Toad Hall."

Lucky Toad gets onto the barge. "So, you're a washerwoman?" asks the woman.

"Oh yes," says Toad, "the best in the country. I'm very good. I love washing!"

"Then I'm very lucky meeting you," says the woman, "I like washing too but I never have the time. There's a big pile of washing inside. You can do my washing."

Toad is frightened. "Oh no! I don't want to ruin your clothes. I usually wash gentlemen's clothes."

"Oh no," says the woman, "I want you to be happy!"

Toad is worried but he thinks, "It can't be so difficult to wash."

Half an hour later Toad is angry. The clothes are still dirty. Suddenly he hears the barge woman. She is laughing. "You can't wash! You aren't a washerwoman!"

Toad is furious! "You common barge woman! I'm Toad. The distinguished Toad! You mustn't laugh at me!"

The woman looks at Toad under his bonnet. "Yes, you are," she cries, "a horrible toad in my nice clean barge!"

She takes him by the legs and throws him into the water. It is very cold. Toad gets out of the water. He looks at the woman. She is laughing at him. Toad wants revenge! [1] He runs after the barge. He takes the horse and gallops [2] away.

"Stop! Stop! Stop!" shouts the woman. Toad laughs.

After some miles Toad and the horse are sleepy and the horse stops to eat some grass. Toad looks around. He sees an old, dirty gypsy caravan. There is a man sitting next to it. There is also a fire.

---

1. **revenge** : 報復。

2. **gallops** : 飛跑。

Over the fire is a pot [1] full of stew. [2] Toad is very hungry and the stew smells delicious!

The gypsy asks, "Do you want to sell your horse?"

"Oh no," replies Toad, "I love my horse. But how much can you pay me?"

"A shilling [3] a leg," replies the gypsy.

"A shilling a leg?" says Toad, "I must work out [4] how much that is in total." He thinks for a minute. "But that's only four shillings! I cannot accept that. Give me six shillings and some breakfast and you can have my horse."

The gypsy agrees and gives Toad six shillings. Then he gives him an enormous plate of stew. Toad eats and eats and eats. After, the gypsy gives him directions for the river bank and Toad says goodbye.

He is happy again. The sun is shining. He has money in his pockets and a full stomach. And he is near home.

After some time he sees a car in the distance. "Wonderful!" thinks Toad, "I can stop the car and ask for a lift. [5] Then I can return to Toad Hall in a car."

He steps into the road and the car slows down. But suddenly Toad becomes pale and falls to the ground. It is the car from outside the Red Lion. And the people in the car are the same people!

"Oh no! Prison again! Dry bread and water again! What a fool [6] I am!" cries Toad.

The car stops and two men get out. "Oh dear! A washerwoman in the road. Let's take her to the village." They put Toad in the car and

---

1. **pot** :
2. **stew** : 燉的肉和蔬菜。
3. **shilling** : 先令。1先令＝5便士。
4. **work out** : 算出。
5. **lift** : 搭便車。
6. **fool** : 蠢人。

continue along the road.

Toad feels brave again because the men do not recognise him.

"How do you feel now?" asks one of the men.

"Better, thank you, sir," says Toad, "But maybe if I can sit in the front seat next to the driver, I can have some fresh air on my face."

"Very sensible," says the man. So Toad gets into the front seat.

"Please, sir," says Toad, "can I drive the car for a little?"

The driver laughs. "You can try, madam."

Toad gets into the driver's seat and pretends to listen to the driver's instructions. At first he drives very carefully. The two men laugh and applaud, [1] "Just imagine! A washerwoman driving so well!"

Toad goes a little faster, then faster and faster.

The men say, "Be careful, washerwoman!"

This annoys [2] Toad and he loses his head.

"Washerwoman!" he shouts, "I'm Toad, the motor-car thief, the famous, the clever, the fearless Toad!"

The two men jump on Toad and the car goes off the road and finishes up in a pond. [3]

Toad flies through the air and lands on the soft grass of a meadow.

He gets up and starts to run. "Ho! Ho!" he cries, "Toad wins again! Clever Toad!" He looks behind him. He sees the driver and two policemen running after him.

"What an idiot I am," he cries while he runs, "How stupid I am!"

He runs and runs but they get nearer. Poor Toad! He is a fat animal and his legs are short.

Suddenly he falls into water. He is in the river! The water carries him along and soon he sees a big hole in the river bank. He takes hold

1. **applaud**：鼓掌。

2. **annoys**：惹惱。

3. **pond**：

and pulls himself out of the water. He looks into the hole and sees a familiar face – brown and small. It is the Water Rat!

Toad tries to tell Rat about his adventures and about how clever he is but Rat is very serious. "Toad, you are very silly. You must try to be sensible and mustn't embarrass your friends."

Toad is very sorry. "You're right, Ratty," he says, "I want to be a good Toad in the future. Let's have coffee and then I can go to Toad Hall and get some clean clothes."

"Go to Toad Hall?" cries Rat, "Don't you know?"

Toad becomes pale. "Know what, Ratty?"

"You don't know about the ferrets and the weasels? They're living in Toad Hall. They think you aren't coming back from prison. They lie in bed half the day and eat your food and drink your drink. The place is in a mess." [1]

Toad gets up and takes a stick.

"It's no good," says Rat, "They've got sentries [2] and are armed. You must wait."

But Toad doesn't want to wait. He marches down the road to Toad Hall. At the front gate there is a ferret. He shoots at Toad and so Toad runs back to Rat.

Badger and Mole arrive. "We can't attack the house," says Badger, "They're too strong. But there's a tunnel; it goes from the river bank to the middle of Toad Hall. Tomorrow night it's the chief weasel's birthday and there's a big party in the dining room. We can enter secretly and then run into the dining room with our pistols and swords."

"Yes! Yes!" cries Toad happily.

"Now, it's time to go to bed," says Badger, "We must rest because we have got a lot of work to do tomorrow night."

---

1. **in a mess** : 一團糟。　　　　　　2. **sentries** : 門衛。

UNDERSTANDING THE TEXT

1 **Are these sentences "Right" (A) or "Wrong" (B)? If there is not enough information to answer "Right" or "Wrong", choose "Doesn't say" (C).**

1 The barge woman offers to take Toad near to Toad Hall.
   A Right   **B** Wrong   **C** Doesn't say

2 Toad offers to wash the barge woman's clothes.
   A Right   **B** Wrong   **C** Doesn't say

3 The barge woman calls the police after Toad steals the horse.
   A Right   **B** Wrong   **C** Doesn't say

4 The gypsy gives Toad 4 shillings for the horse.
   A Right   **B** Wrong   **C** Doesn't say

5 The two men in the car recognise Toad.
   A Right   **B** Wrong   **C** Doesn't say

6 Toad drives the car and has an accident.
   A Right   **B** Wrong   **C** Doesn't say

7 Rat wants to hear about all of Toad's adventures.
   A Right   **B** Wrong   **C** Doesn't say

8 The ferrets and weasels are living in Toad Hall now.
   A Right   **B** Wrong   **C** Doesn't say

2 **A SHILLING A LEG**
Use the words in the box to fill the gaps.

divided by   minus   multiplied by   equals   plus

1 Six times three .... eighteen.
2 Five .... five equals ten.
3 Nine .... two equals seven.
4 Twelve .... three equals four.
5 One .... four equals four.

3 **Complete the conversations. Choose A, B or C.**

1 Are you Toad of Toad Hall?

    A ☐ Yes, I do.
    B ☐ Not at all!
    C ☐ Yes, of course!

2 How is Badger?

    A ☐ Big and black.
    B ☐ Much better.
    C ☐ In the Wild Wood.

3 Hello, this is Mole speaking. Is that Rat?

    A ☐ No, I'm not.
    B ☐ Yes, speaking.
    C ☐ Yes, I am.

BEFORE YOU READ

1 **VOCABULARY**

Do you know these words? Match the words in the box to the pictures.

> sword   truncheon   flask   pistol
> handcuffs   lantern

CHAPTER 8

THE RETURN OF MR TOAD

he following evening Rat calls everyone into the sitting
room and prepares them for the expedition. [1] He gives
them a belt, [2] a sword, a pair of pistols, a policeman's
truncheon, handcuffs, a flask and a sandwich box.

When they are ready, Badger takes a lantern and says,
"Now follow me! Mole first, then Rat and Toad last. And Toady, don't
talk!" Toad wants to be part of the expedition so he is quiet.

Badger takes them along the river for a little way and then goes into
a hole in the river bank. Mole and Rat follow silently but Toad slips
and falls into the water with a loud splash. His friends pull him out

1. **expedition** : 探險。

2. **belt** :

but Badger is very angry. They continue along the secret tunnel. It is cold and dark and poor Toad starts to shiver [1] because he is frightened and also because he is completely wet.

At last Badger says, "We must be under the Hall now." They are at the end of the tunnel. There is a door and they all push against it. It opens and they are in the pantry [2] next to the dining room.

The weasels are making a lot of noise. They hear the chief weasel say, "Thank you, thank you, but before I finish I would like to say one word about our kind host, Mr Toad; good, modest, honest Toad!" Everybody laughs and Toad is furious!

Badger stands up, takes his stick and says, "The time is come! Follow me!"

They open the door and the four friends run into the dining room. The weasels and ferrets are terrified and run everywhere in a panic. The four friends go up and down the room hitting the animals with their sticks, and the weasels and ferrets try to escape through the windows and up the chimney. [3] After five minutes the room is empty.

"Now, Toad," says Badger, "we've got your house back for you. Now you can get us some food. I'm hungry."

Toad is a little offended because Badger doesn't tell him "well done" and "you are a great fighter", but he says nothing and finds some food for them to eat.

The next morning Toad wakes up late as usual. He comes down for breakfast. Rat and Mole are sitting in the garden and Badger is in the armchair reading the newspaper.

"Toad," says Badger, "you must have a banquet to celebrate your return and you must write the invitations now."

---

1. **shiver** : 顫抖。
2. **pantry** : 配膳間。
3. **chimney** : 煙囪。

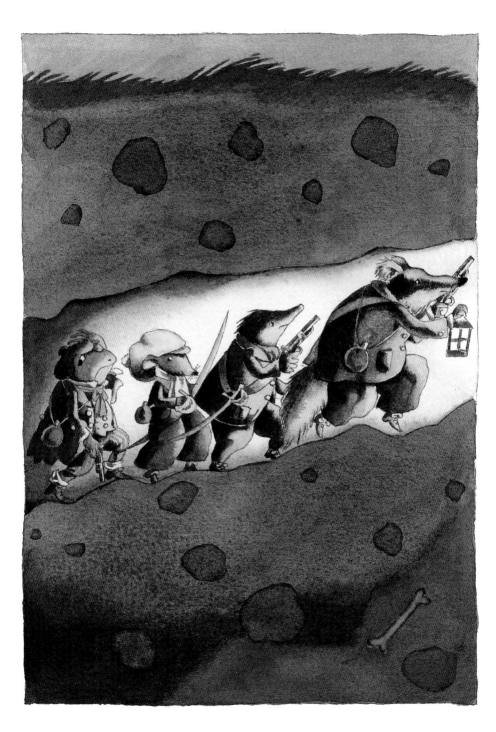

"What?!" cries Toad, "I must stay inside and write letters on a lovely morning like this!"

But then Toad has an idea. "But wait! Of course, dear Badger, I can start immediately." Toad wants to write about his important part in the fight and also about his many adventures. He also thinks he can give a speech [1] and sing some songs at the banquet.

He works hard all morning and when a weasel knocks at the door at midday and asks if he can be of service, Toad tells him to deliver [2] the invitations.

1. **speech** : 演講。

2. **deliver** : 遞送。

THE RETURN OF MR TOAD

But after lunch Rat and Badger sit Toad in a chair. "Look, Toad," says Rat, "you must understand – you can't give a speech or sing songs."

"Can't I sing just one little song?" asks Toad.

"No!" says Rat. "You know that your songs are all boasting and vanity, and your speeches are gross exaggeration. You know you must change."

"You're right. I promise to be a different Toad. But this is a hard world!"

That evening when the banquet begins, Toad enters the dining room to meet his guests. All the animals cheer [1] and congratulate him

1. **cheer** : 歡呼。

but Toad is very humble. "Oh no," he says, "Badger, Rat and Mole are the real heroes."

The animals are very puzzled [1] by his behaviour and Toad is happy because he feels that everyone is very interested in him.

At the end of the evening some animals ask for a speech and a song but Toad shakes his head. [2]

He is a changed Toad!

After this great adventure the four animals continue their lives in joy and contentment. Toad sends a gold chain and locket [3] with pearls to the gaoler's daughter with a modest and grateful letter.

The train driver also receives thanks and compensation. And Badger also makes Toad send money to the barge woman for her horse.

Sometimes during the long summer evenings the friends go for a walk in the Wild Wood. The weasels greet them with respect. Mother weasels call their children, point and say, "Look! There goes great Mr Toad, the brave Rat and famous Mr Mole." But when their children are naughty [4] they say that the terrible grey Badger is coming to get them. This is, of course, not true because Badger is very fond of children; but it always has an effect.

1. **puzzled** : 困惑。
2. **shakes his head** : 搖頭。
3. **gold ... locket** :
4. **naughty** : 淘氣。

UNDERSTANDING THE TEXT

1 **Choose A, B or C.**

1 Why is Toad quiet?
   A ☐ Because he wants to take part in the expedition.
   B ☐ Because he is last.
   C ☐ Because he isn't talking.

2 Badger is angry because
   A ☐ Mole and Rat follow silently.
   B ☐ Toad is slow.
   C ☐ Toad makes a lot of noise.

3 The tunnel opens into the
   A ☐ dining room.
   B ☐ hall.
   C ☐ pantry.

4 When the four friends run into the dining room,
   A ☐ the weasels fight back.
   B ☐ no one is there.
   C ☐ the weasels run away.

5 At the banquet
   A ☐ Toad behaves in his usual way.
   B ☐ Toad is very humble.
   C ☐ Toad boasts about his adventures.

2 **Read Toad's invitation to the banquet and choose A, B or C for each space.**

You are (1)................ to a banquet this evening (2)................ Toad Hall.
Please (3)................ elegantly.
Programme:
• Speeches (4)................ Toad about his great (5)................:
  The prison system – the waterways of old England – horse buying and selling – property
• Songs by Toad
  The banquet (6)................ at 8 o'clock.

1	**A** invited	**B** expected	**C** asked
2	**A** in	**B** at	**C** to
3	**A** dress	**B** clothe	**C** wear
4	**A** about	**B** of	**C** by
5	**A** trips	**B** adventures	**C** travel
6	**A** starts	**B** finishes	**C** beginns

65

EXIT TEST 1

1 **Match the descriptions to the correct character.**

A Mole   **B** Rat   **C** Badger   **D** Toad

1 ☐ He changes hobby all the time.
2 ☐ He lives in the Wild Wood.
3 ☐ He invites Mole to stay with him.
4 ☐ He lives on the river bank.
5 ☐ He doesn't like being in company.
6 ☐ He gets lost in the Wild Wood.
7 ☐ He isn't very clever.
8 ☐ He likes cars.
9 ☐ He escapes from Toad Hall.
10 ☐ He has got a boat.
11 ☐ He has a plan to liberate Toad Hall from the weasels and ferrets.
12 ☐ He likes Badger's underground house.

KET

2 **Are these sentences "Right" (A) or "Wrong" (B)? If there is not enough information to answer "Right" or "Wrong", choose "Doesn't say" (C).**

1 Mole meets Rat on the river bank.
A Right   **B** Wrong   **C** Doesn't say

2 Mole has got a boat.
A Right   **B** Wrong   **C** Doesn't say

3 Toad changes hobby all the time.
A Right   **B** Wrong   **C** Doesn't say

4 When Mole and Rat arrive Badger is sleeping.
A Right   **B** Wrong   **C** Doesn't say

5 Badger, Mole and Rat want to help Toad.
A Right   **B** Wrong   **C** Doesn't say

6 Toad stops being interested in cars.
A Right   **B** Wrong   **C** Doesn't say

7   Toad eats his lunch at the Red Lion inn.
    A Right   **B** Wrong   **C** Doesn't say

8   The gaoler's daughter helps Toad.
    A Right   **B** Wrong   **C** Doesn't say

9   The washerwoman gives Toad her clothes for free.
    A Right   **B** Wrong   **C** Doesn't say

10 The barge woman throws Toad into the water.
    A Right   **B** Wrong   **C** Doesn't say

11 Badger has an idea of how to free Toad Hall.
    A Right   **B** Wrong   **C** Doesn't say

12 Toad doesn't change after his adventures.
    A Right   **B** Wrong   **C** Doesn't say

 Match the words to their definitions.

1	someone who lives near you	**A**	guilty
2	bad person	**B**	lift
3	pub	**C**	naughty
4	responsible for something illegal	**D**	villain
5	say no to	**E**	refuse
6	free journey in a car	**F**	inn
7	organised journey	**G**	expedition
8	bad	**H**	neighbour

EXIT TEST 2

 Choose the correct answer A, B or C.

1. Mole's house is
   A. underground.   **B.** in a meadow.   **C.** in a tunnel.

2. Toad's first hobby was
   A. cycling.   **B.** sailing.   **C.** houseboating.

3. Toad, Rat and Badger set off
   A. in the morning.   **B.** in the afternoon.   **C.** in the evening.

4. Mole decides to go to the Wild Wood
   A. to meet Otter.   **B.** because Rat sleeps a lot.
   C. to meet Badger.

5. Rat and Mole stay at Badger's house for
   A. two nights.   **B.** a week.   **C.** one night.

6. Badger, Rat and Mole lock Toad
   A. in his bedroom.   **B.** in his car.   **C.** in his hall.

7. Toad is sent to prison for
   A. two years.   **B.** twenty years.   **C.** twelve years.

8. Who is Toad's friend in the prison?
   A. the gaoler's daughter   **B.** the gaoler   **C.** the washerwoman

9. The barge woman throws Toad into the water because
   A. he takes her horse.
   B. he doesn't wash her clothes.   **C.** he is a toad.

10. At the banquet
    A. Toad sings some songs.
    B. Toad gives a speech.   **C.** Toad is humble.

 Read the definitions. What is the word for each one? The first letter is already there. There is one space for each other letter in the word.

1. a group of trees   w _ _ _
2. the hottest season   s _ _ _ _ _
3. many animals do this in winter   m _ _ _ _ _ _
4. you wear this when it's cold   c _ _ _
5. a policemen carries one of these   t _ _ _ _ _ _ _ _
6. a field with grass   m _ _ _ _ _
7. the light that comes from the sun   s _ _ _ _ _ _ _
8. a type of boat   b _ _ _ _

The Wind in the Willows

KEY TO THE EXERCISES AND EXIT TESTS

INTRODUCTION

Page 11, exercise 2

1 willow **2** grass **3** meadow
4 wood **5** river **6** sunlight
7 river bank

Page 11, exercise 3

CHAPTER 1

Page 16, exercise 1

1 A **2** B **3** A **4** A **5** C **6** A **7** B **8** B

Page 16, exercise 2

1 C **2** B **3** A

Page 17, exercise 3

A 1 spring **2** winter **3** autumn
  4 summer
B spring – flowers, rain
  winter – cold, ice skating, skiing,
  coats, snow
  autumn – leaves, gold, yellow
  summer – hot, beach, swimming, ice
  cream, holidays
C

summer   autumn

spring   winter

CHAPTER 2

Page 22, exercise 1

1 B 2 B 3 B 4 A 5 C 6 A 7 A 8 B

Page 22, exercise 2

Open answer.

CHAPTER 3

Page 28, exercise 1

1 Badger.
2 Because it's winter time.
3 Because he sees hundreds of faces with hard eyes.
4 He takes two pistols and a big stick.
5 It's snowing.
6 They find Badger's house.

Page 28, exercise 2

1 B 2 D 3 C 4 G 5 F

Page 28, exercise 3

Open answer.

ANIMALS IN WINTER

Page 30, exercise 1

1 fur 2 migrate 3 energy 4 store
5 hibernation 6 heartbeat

CHAPTER 4

Page 31, exercise 1

1 B 2 A 3 B 4 B 5 B

Page 31, exercise 2

A angry **B** sensible **C** sleepy
D happy **E** good

1 angry 2 good 3 sensible 4 sleepy
5 happy

Page 35, exercise 1

1 A 2 A 3 C 4 B 5 B 6 B

Page 35, exercise 2

1 Who 2 How 3 Where 4 When
5 Why

CHAPTER 5

Page 40, exercise 1

1 B 2 A 3 B 4 A 5 A 6 A 7 C

Page 40, exercise 2

1 am 2 in 3 a 4 and 5 very 6 I
7 are 8 me 9 do

Page 41, exercise 3

1 It's half past two./ It's two thirty.
2 It's midnight. /It's midday./It's twelve o'clock.
3 It's three o'clock.
4 It's a quarter to six./It's five forty-five.
5 It's a quarter past ten./It's ten fifteen.
6 It's twenty-five past five./It's five twenty-five.

CHAPTER 6

Page 48, exercise 1

1 Because she is very fond of animals and is sorry for Toad.
2 He talks about his home and his friends.
3 He thinks that she is in love with him.
4 She gives Toad a cotton dress, an apron and a bonnet.
5 He gives her a pile of gold coins.
6 Because he has no money.
7 Because he is sorry for Toad.
8 He jumps after the tunnel.

Page 48, exercise 2

1 goggles 2 gloves 3 shoes 4 shirt
5 jacket 6 waistcoat 7 trousers
8 coat 9 bonnet 10 dress 11 apron

Chapter 7

Page 57, exercise 1

1 A   2 B   3 C   4 B   5 B   6 A   7 B   8 A

Page 57, exercise 2

1 equals   2 plus   3 minus   4 divided by   5 multiplied by

Page 58, exercise 3

1 C   2 B   3 B

Chapter 8

Page 58, exercise 1

1 flask   2 handcuffs   3 lantern   4 sword   5 pistol   6 truncheon

Page 65, exercise 1

1 A   2 C   3 C   4 C   5 B

Page 65, exercise 2

1 A   2 B   3 A   4 C   5 B   6 A

KEY TO EXIT TEST 1

Page 66, exercise 1

1D / 2C / 3B / 4B / 5C / 6A / 7D / 8D / 9D / 10B / 11C / 12A

Page 66, exercise 2

1A / 2B / 3A / 4C / 5A / 6B / 7C / 8A / 9B / 10A / 11A / 12B

Page 67, exercise 3

1H / 2D / 3F / 4A / 5E / 6B / 7G / 8C

KEY TO EXIT TEST 2

Page 68, exercise 1

1 A   2 B   3 B   4 C   5 C   6 A   7 B   8 A   9 C   10 C

Page 68, exercise 2

1 wood   2 summer   3 migrate   4 coat   5 truncheon
6 meadow   7 sunshine   8 barge

NOTES

NOTES

NOTES

Black Cat English Readers

BLACK CAT ENGLISH CLUB

Membership Application Form

BLACK CAT ENGLISH CLUB is for those who love English reading and seek for better English to share and learn with fun together.

Benefits offered:
    - Membership Card
    - Member badge, poster, bookmark
    - Book discount coupon
    - Black Cat English Reward Scheme
    - English learning e-forum
    - Surprise gift and more...

Simply fill out the application form below and fax it back to **2565 1113**.

Join Now! It's FREE exclusively for readers who have purchased *Black Cat English Readers* !

The book(or book set) that you have purchased: _____

English Name: _____ (Surname) _____ (Given Name)

Chinese Name: _____

Address: _____

Tel: _____ Fax: _____

Email: _____
Sex: ❏ Male   ❏ Female   (Login password for e-forum will be sent to this email address.)

Education Background: ❏ Primary 1-3   ❏ Primary 4-6   ❏ Junior Secondary Education (F1-3)
            ❏ Senior Secondary Education (F4-5)   ❏ Matriculation
            ❏ College   ❏ University or above

Age: ❏ 6 - 9   ❏ 10 - 12   ❏ 13 - 15   ❏ 16 - 18   ❏ 19 - 24   ❏ 25 - 34
    ❏ 35 - 44   ❏ 45 - 54   ❏ 55 or above

Occupation: ❏ Student   ❏ Teacher   ❏ White Collar   ❏ Blue Collar
           ❏ Professional   ❏ Manager   ❏ Business Owner   ❏ Housewife
           ❏ Others (please specify: _____)

As a member, what would you like **BLACK CAT ENGLISH CLUB** to offer:
    ❏ Member gathering/ party   ❏ English class with native teacher   ❏ English competition
    ❏ Newsletter   ❏ Online sharing   ❏ Book fair
    ❏ Book discount   ❏ Others (please specify: _____)

Other suggestions to **BLACK CAT ENGLISH CLUB**:

_____

Please sign here: _____

(Date: _____)